EVYN HUNTER AND THE SECRET INVASION

PATRICK NIGHT

Evyn Hunter and the Secret Invasion

This is a work of fiction. All of the characters, names, incidents, organizations, and dialogue in this novel are either the products of the author's imagination or are used fictitiously.

iUniverse books may be ordered through booksellers or by contacting:

iUniverse
1663 Liberty Drive
Bloomington, IN 47403
www.iuniverse.com
1-800-Authors (1-800-288-4677)

ISBN: 978-1-4917-5920-2 (sc)
ISBN: 978-1-4917-5919-6 (e)

Library of Congress Control Number: 2015903137

Print information available on the last page.

iUniverse rev. date: 3/31/2015

EVYN HUNTER AND THE
AND THE
SECRET
INVASION

CONTENTS

CHAPTER 1

EVYN HUNTER

This story begins on a beautiful, sunny morning in the small city of Newport. Just minutes down the highway from the big city of Los Angeles, this quiet suburban city is nestled comfortably out of the way, between the hills and the ocean.

Rows of bright yellow school buses line up in front of Sir Arthur Wilfred High School, dropping students off as they have every morning for the entire school year. The students eagerly make their way across the school grounds, chatting and laughing, happy that the grueling week of school is almost over, and looking forward to the upcoming weekend.

The sun is shining bright and warm on the school buses as they unload the students, some of which are still just waking up. One, in particular, is me, Evyn Hunter.

Seemingly, I am an ordinary thirteen-year-old boy in the crowd of kids now making their way toward the school. As far as anyone can tell, I am an average teenager. I'm not as big as the other boys my age—not quite as tall or as fast or as strong, and definitely not as cool with the girls as some of the other boys. My dirty-blond hair is cut short and trimmed nicely, just like everyone else's. I love hanging out with my friends, playing sports, watching television and movies, playing video games, and listening to my favorite music. I am a happy-go-lucky character, and I'm content with my average life.

What sets me apart from everyone else—what makes me special—is that I have an interesting and mysterious future ahead of me. I will soon find out—unknown to anyone, including myself—that I am destined for greatness.

The new high school was built just a few years ago to accommodate the large number of kids who now live in the city. The fancy new building with its three floors of clean brick, large windows, and elegant glass doors is an amazing sight. The old building—which has since been converted into an office building with its old brown bricks, cracked pavement, and tacky floors—pales in comparison to this new, state-of-the-art facility. The high school has an indoor swimming pool, a huge gymnasium, and a full-size football field. The cafeteria is large and bright, positioned right next to the library. The school has everything a promising student could possibly need from an education, all under one roof.

There is a sea of students in the hallways, some on their cell phones watching videos or browsing the Internet, others carrying their skateboards in from outside. Some are socializing, most of them enjoying themselves while waiting for the school bell to ring. And there I stand, alone by my locker, in a trance, staring at the lovely Chloe Taylor.

She is so gorgeous, I think.

Chloe is beautiful and charismatic; her piercing green eyes and long, blonde hair always hypnotize me. She only transferred to Sir Arthur Wilfred High earlier in the school year and has already made lots of friends. Although Chloe hasn't realized it yet, she has also captured my eyes and heart, although I have not built up the courage to approach her.

"Dude, you've got to stop torturing yourself!" Sam exclaims

from out of nowhere as he walks up to me and snaps me out of my trance. "Come on, Ev! Let's get to class before we're late, pal."

Sam Desjardins and I first met back in the early days of middle school, when he stood up to a group of bullies who were picking on me. Ever since then, we have been best friends. Sam is much taller and stronger than I am, and much more confident. Although Sam's dark brown hair and big muscles make me a little envious, I look up to him like a big brother. We grew up in the same neighborhood and have gone to the same schools, and we are always there for each other.

Early-morning classes drag on the longest. Every morning, as I try to cast off my lingering sleepiness, I find these first classes of the day the hardest to face. With my best friend, Sam, alongside me, I try to stay awake just long enough to get through the boring computer class and geography lessons. Although Sam's private classroom antics keep me smiling and entertained, nothing comes as such a joy as knowing that lunchtime is just around the corner.

The mystery of the lunchroom is understood by every student at Sir Arthur Wilfred High School yet never spoken about. The older students sit at the back of the cafeteria, near the large exit doors, while the youngest students are forced to eat way up front beside the busy crowd of students lining up to get their food. The older students eat together, and the younger students eat together; they don't mix. The crowds of middle students all stay at the middle tables, trying to avoid the youngest students and trying to remain unnoticed by the older ones. This is how lunch at school has always been and will always be, accepted and unquestioned for years, and I am about to find out why you don't go against the traditions of the lunchroom.

As Sam and I wait patiently in line for food, a group of older kids comes bumping and shoving their way up the line.

"Those guys have no respect. Someone should teach them some manners," Sam whispers to me.

"No cutting in line, you gorillas!" I mean to only mutter under my breath, but I blurt out the remark louder than expected.

"I didn't mean for *you* to teach them manners, Evyn." Sam is shocked by my remark.

One of the older students overhears the rude comment and turns his head slowly toward us and glares at me. "Did you say something?" he says.

I was not expecting anyone to hear me, nor did I want to cause any sort of trouble with the older boys. Luckily for me, a teacher just happens to be walking by and sees the confrontation before it escalates. The older boy notices the teacher watching, so he just gives me a quick scowl and walks away.

"Hey, Evyn, look who's right over there!" Sam comments as we take a seat in the lunchroom. Sitting just a few tables away are Chloe and a few of her friends. "Why don't you go talk to her?" Sam pushes, knowing how much I like her.

"Yeah, right, why would she ever want to talk to me?" I humbly reply.

"Have a little confidence, man. Just go ask her if she's enjoying her lunch, and let the conversation go from there." Sam continues to try to help me with some friendly advice.

"As usual, Sam, your advice sounds great, and thanks a lot, but I'm just not sure. You make it sound so easy."

"You only live once, buddy. I'm just trying to help."

I look over at Chloe and recall the first time I met her—well, I didn't really *meet* her. She walked into my homeroom class a few minutes past the bell. Chloe seemed to enter the classroom in slow motion, as my heart skipped a beat at the first sight of her. Her rosy complexion and movie-star smile took me by surprise. She was the most beautiful girl I had ever seen. Admittance papers in hand, her backpack draped over her shoulder, her long, beautiful blonde hair slowly waving in the air-conditioned room and bouncing as she walked, she took the open seat in front of my desk. I tried to swallow the lump out of my throat but found it impossible to form a single word, let alone a whole sentence.

"So are you going to talk to her or what?" Sam's question pulls me reluctantly from my daydream and back to the lunchroom table, leaving me somewhat disappointed. After several moments, I finally build up the courage to speak to Chloe. I figure I might as well swallow my pride and just get it over with. *What's the worst thing that could happen?* I say to myself.

I slowly stand up from the table and toss my tray of garbage into one of the large garbage bins as I walk toward Chloe.

Little do I realize that at the other end of the cafeteria the group of older boys from earlier are all finished with their food and feeling rowdy. Seeing me all alone, making my way toward Chloe, the tough, angry boy, who almost let me have it in the lunch line decides to make an example of me.

Now just a few steps away from Chloe, I quietly call out to her. "Hey, Chloe, how are-"

I am cut off midsentence. Just as Chloe turns to see who is talking to her, the older boy steps directly in between Chloe and me, saying, "Hey, there, squirt; no time to talk to the cute girls. You forgot to toss out your garbage!"

The rude announcement from the bully is not meant to be taken seriously. Everyone within hearing distance is now paying attention, some with cell-phone cameras in hand, already recording the scene that is about to unfold.

"Actually, I just did throw out my garbage, thanks. Excuse me," I hopelessly reply.

"No, no, no, you really don't get it. I think you need a reminder of how to respect your elders," the bully snidely remarks as he gets a little closer to me.

"What are you talking about?" I ask helplessly. I am cut off yet again and taken by surprise.

The much larger boy reaches out and swiftly grabs me, holding one arm around my waist and easily scooping me up with the other.

He carries me, squirming and kicking to get free, several steps away from Chloe and her friends. He tosses me into the large garbage bin, rolling me in gross leftover lunches, old food wrappers, rotten food, and humiliation. The garbage doesn't bother me nearly as much as the sheer embarrassment of it all.

How am I ever going to live this down? I think.

"Maybe now you'll think twice before talking back!" The bully calls his parting words of advice over his shoulder as he walks away, laughing.

The day drags on after the humiliating lunchroom fiasco. There is math after English and science before phys ed, and I just can't wait for this day to be over. I keep thinking about how much I hate cell phones, which I never realized until now. All I want to do is get home and try to live down the embarrassment I faced in front of Chloe.

The rest of the day is just a blurry, boring blend of teachers talking, pencils scratching on paper, and students walking by faster than I can focus on them. A large black hole of shock encircles my ego. The only resounding thought left in my head is of what an awful impression I must have made on Chloe and how little she must think of me. But my day isn't over yet.

Standing on the gymnasium floor like a department-store mannequin, sporting gym shorts and a T-shirt with the school logo on it, I still can't stop thinking of Chloe. All of a sudden, a volleyball strikes me on the side of my head, abruptly knocking me to the gym floor.

"Could my day get any worse?" I grumble to myself from the gymnasium floor.

A few snickers and hints of laughter spring forward from everyone in the gym who witnessed the sudden strike. A small group of girls in the bleachers watching with their cell phones in hand exclaim quietly as they point and laugh. "That's the kid in the video from lunchtime," one says.

"Come on, Evyn; wake up, and get in the game!" the phys ed teacher shouts from the side of the gymnasium.

Sam, playing alongside me, helps me to my feet and asks, "Evyn, are you feeling okay? You're supposed to use your hands for volleyball and your head for math class."

Still embarrassed, I try to reply to Sam's funny comment. "Yeah, I'm fine. At least Chloe's not watching."

"You can't keep letting that bother you. There will always be someone who wants to see you fail when they see you trying to succeed at something. At least you tried to stand up to that bully and talk to Chloe," Sam replies with a smile.

I smile at the support I can count on from Sam. Ahead of his years, Sam has a wise and confident outlook on life.

Most days, my favorite class is history, as it's the last class of the day. I enjoy the stories and the insight into worlds gone by, hearing about early American settlers and wars fought between countries of the world. It keeps me intrigued. In this class, I can unwind and forget any troubles I may have faced throughout the day, but today, I sit, staring at the clock.

The clock's hands move slowly, click by click, counting the seconds and minutes until the end of the school day. I sit there, anticipating the beloved dismissal bell's ringing, looking at the clock for what seems like forever. What feels like a lifetime is spent watching the clock, so much so that the hands almost tick backward as anticipation builds. My heart rate picks up; I can feel the hairs on the back of my neck stand on end.

Three, two, one—the dismissal bell echoes resoundingly throughout the entire school. Never have I so badly wanted a day to end. I pick up my school books, toss them into my backpack, and start off out of the school quicker than anyone. I do not stop by my locker, chat with any friends, or even say good-bye to Sam before banging open the school's large front doors and running home.

CHAPTER 2

STRANGE OCCURRENCES

My long walk home is almost over when I turn onto the last short road and spot a man standing on the corner. The man is dressed in a dark suit, complete with a dark overcoat; a large, dark, brimmed hat; and black sunglasses, hiding his face. Normally, I wouldn't think anything of him, but today seems exceptionally hot to be wearing such a heavy suit.

My curiosity shifts to a quiet sense of fear as the man lifts his head and looks straight into my eyes. The man's gaze seems very curious, as if, for some reason, he is specifically looking for me. Suddenly, the man starts walking toward me. *Why would this strange man be looking for me, and what could he possibly want?* I think. *I've never seen him before in my life.*

As if my day hasn't been bad enough already, the last thing I want to do is find out what this man in the dark suit wants. I brush off any concerns and go in the opposite direction, heading for the alleyway, a shortcut to my house.

I make it down the alley, hop a small chain-link fence, and pop out at the top of my street. I head straight for home, not looking back for a second. Since leaving the school, I've had a strange feeling

I was being followed, but until now, I didn't think anything of it. Seeing the man in a dark suit, a slight feeling of fear overwhelms me. So close to home yet feeling so far from safety, I feel a looming presence all around me. Someone is standing right behind me.

Then, like the sweet voice of an angel, soft and serene, from behind me come the most beautiful, melodic words I have ever heard. "Hey, it was really cool of you to try to talk to me today." It is Chloe. She has been trying to catch up with me ever since I left school in a hurry.

When I turn around, I am so surprised to see Chloe that I can barely muster two words. "Excuse me?"

As I try to comprehend what's happening, Chloe continues. "It was really stupid—what that guy did to you at school. He's such a jerk. I felt really bad about not catching up to you right after."

Trying with all my nervous might to say something witty, I respond without really thinking. "Oh, that's okay. I can handle that guy. I hear his mom's been feeding him steroids in his breakfast for years."

I manage to get a small laugh out of Chloe, and then she smiles.

"If you're not too busy this weekend, maybe you would like to come hang out at the mall with me."

I am so amazed—shocked to hear these magical words I have always longed to hear. It takes a second to register in my head, but I manage to respond without sounding too desperate. "Yes. Definitely."

"Great. How about tomorrow?" Chloe asks with a smile.

"Tomorrow sounds perfect."

"Okay, meet me in the food court around noon."

"Great, I'll see you tomorrow."

I wait until Chloe leaves before cracking the biggest smile my face has ever shown. I jump for joy, celebrating my first real encounter with Chloe, and I completely forget the embarrassment I faced early in the day and my odd encounter with the man in the dark suit.

I wake up in the morning with a spring in my step. I am overjoyed at my expectations of the day ahead and excited to spend it at the mall with Chloe. I head down the street toward the big shopping mall. The mall is quite far, taking me out of my suburban neighborhood, past all the shops on Main Street, beyond the high school, and almost downtown. I don't mind the walk at all. The fact that Chloe even talked to me—let alone asked me to hang out this Saturday—blows my mind.

The famous Fashion Island Mall, a beacon of architectural achievement, sets itself apart from all other buildings in the city. Its immense size holds three stories in an open-concept plaza design and houses galleries, boutiques, a grocery store, restaurants, and offices. Fashion Island is the biggest shopping mall for miles. Many people do their shopping on the weekend so they don't have to do it during the week, so, of all days, the mall seems busiest on Saturdays. There are so many entertaining activities to do at Fashion Island. There's a small roller coaster, a movie theater, an arcade, and an endless number of restaurants surrounding the large food court.

I walk into the mall through the large glass doors, opening them with ease, considering their immense size. As I enter, I am taken aback by how many people are shopping today. There are shoppers everywhere, moving about this way and that in an unorganized mess of misdirection. I take a breath and join them.

Bunched into the crowded mall, I slowly make it to the escalator and take a slow ride up to the third-floor food court.

The food court bustles with hungry people. There are long lines at every restaurant counter. I manage to spot Chloe through the crowds of people. Like a beautiful lighthouse amid the dark sea of people, Chloe can easily be seen, sitting at a table in the food court. I walk over to her without hesitation.

"Hey, how are you?" I politely ask with a smile.

"I'm great, thanks, and you?" she responds.

"Have you been here a long time?"

"No, I just got here. It sure is crowded today."

Next to the food court are the movie theater and the arcade. Chloe and I decide to grab lunch and see a movie. The wait for food is not too long, considering how many people fill the busy food court.

A lot of kids from school spend their Saturdays at the mall. As Chloe and I enjoy chatting over lunch, I spot the group of nasty older boys from school hanging out across the food court. I pretend not to notice them until I see them coming toward us with their usual smirks and evil grins.

As the boys pass, one stops and makes a rude comment. "Aw, look, the little stinker is all cleaned up." The bully is clearly proud of himself, referring to my humiliating visit with the cafeteria garbage bin.

"Aren't you two cute, like a match made in dork heaven," the bully remarks as the older boys all break out in laughter.

Chloe responds instantly. "Don't you idiots have anything better to do than pick on people?"

Everyone in the food court hears Chloe's loud remark. In disappointment, they all stop and look at the older boys, watching for what they will do next. Some fathers and even a couple of security guards overhear Chloe's loud outburst and turn their attention to the bullies as well.

The rude boys no longer have a single word to say. They walk away, obviously feeling embarrassed. I smile at Chloe, and she knows she has impressed me very much.

Over Chloe's shoulder, I can see everyone dismiss the outburst. They quickly lose interest and carry on with their business. But just then, I notice the same man in the dark suit I saw on my way home from school. He is accompanied by another man in almost-identical attire.

The men continue to stare at me long after everyone else loses interest. They are not wearing the most practical clothes for the warm climate and seem very out of place. I find it coincidental that I've seen the first man twice in two days. I am curious but do not pay too much attention to the overdressed men; instead, I carry on having a great time with Chloe. Then we finish our lunch and head to the movie theater.

The movie theater has a modern and elegant front entrance, which matches the shopping mall, and it opens up to a classic movie-theater lobby. The wall is lined with enormous movie posters for coming attractions, and a huge marquee displays all the movies currently being shown. Across the vast, red-carpeted lobby stands a ticket booth and a large, busy snack counter, wafting the inviting smell of fresh, buttered popcorn into the mall.

Chloe and I decide to see the latest romantic comedy. Once we pay for our tickets, the usher outside our selected theater rips our tickets and offers a courteous remark that we enjoy the show. We do just that. Chloe and I have a great time watching the movie, laughing at all the funny scenes at the same time and commenting on all the scenes we either do or do not enjoy.

Partway through the film, I offer to go get snacks. I exit the movie and walk along the red-carpeted floors to the snack counter. Having waited until the movie was under way, I find that the lines are much shorter than before. In no time at all, I happily order a large popcorn and two soft drinks.

I make my way back into the dark theater and scan the rows of people, trying to remember where I left Chloe. Then, amid all the people, above the noise of the feature playing on the massive screen, I hear Chloe's lovely voice beckoning to me.

"Evyn, over here!" Chloe happily calls out.

"Sh!"

"She's right there, Evyn!"

"Shut up!"

Chloe is met with all sorts of rude comments from the movie-theater patrons. Avid moviegoers have no patience for distractions or interruptions during a film.

Chloe sinks back into her seat, slightly embarrassed by her outburst, not realizing how loud she could be. She felt as if it were just her and me enjoying the movie. No one else really matters to her at this moment. I make my way down the row, smiling, and take my seat next to Chloe.

"That was hilarious, Chloe," I whisper, smiling at her.

"No, it wasn't. It was embarrassing," she replies.

"Well, I thought it was really cute. Don't worry about it; they're just strangers," I assure her.

We share the large, overpriced popcorn, and Chloe holds my hand through a sad part of the movie. The touching show of affection warms my heart more than the sad movie scene.

The film reaches its climax. The stars of the film realize how much they love each other and that they can't live without each other—a typical romantic comedy turnaround, but it still pulls on Chloe's heartstrings. She looks over to see if I feel the same about the emotional scene and notices I'm staring right back at her. For a moment, we just gaze into each other's eyes, but then Chloe slowly leans in, closer to me, so I lean toward her and slightly tilt my head.

"Isn't it great how they finally saw the errors of their ways?" Chloe asks him.

"Uh, yeah, it sure was nice to see them get back together," I answer, though I haven't really been paying attention to anything but Chloe throughout the movie.

Excitement erupts in both of us as the stars onscreen share a passionate kiss. Chloe's emotions come to a boiling point, and we lean in toward each other more closely than ever. Chloe and I share our first kiss. Time seems to come to a halt as Chloe's soft lips press against mine. The theater full of people fades away, and nothing else matters. We get lost in our own little world, kissing each other for quite a while. The credits begin to roll as we pull back from each other, smiling and impressed. Neither of us has ever felt anything quite this wonderful. The awkward moment remains the highlight of the movie for both of us, as everyone around us has already exited the theater.

We are the last to exit the movie theater. Neither of us is in any kind of rush for our first date to come to an end.

"Come on. Let's do some window-shopping," Chloe suggests outside the theater.

"Yeah, why not? Sounds like fun," I reply, not wanting to leave Chloe's side.

Lost in each other, we are deeply engaged in our conversation. Hanging on to every word the other person says, Chloe and I really enjoy getting to know each other. We spend as much time as we can walking around the large shopping mall.

When we finally leave the mall, the same two mysterious men in dark suits appear behind us, watching us as we walk away through the parking lot. The men stand outside the large front doors of the mall, staring at us for a moment through their black sunglasses. These mysterious men are all too interested in me, and I can't figure out why. Their ominous features, hidden behind the shadows of their dark attire, leave me more curious to their origins than threatened by them.

Are they government men, secret agents of some kind, or perhaps ruthless mercenaries undercover here in Newport to set off a chain of events that will ultimately overthrow the peaceful way of life here? I think. *No, it's just my imagination. It's probably just a coincidence that I've seen these men so much recently; Newport's not a big city.*

Chloe does not realize we are being watched. I turn my attention back to the men in dark suits, who then briefly look at each other outside the shopping mall and share a concerned look before turning around and going back inside. I brush off these strange men as Chloe and I share a long walk home.

CHAPTER 3

GHOST TOWN

My alarm goes off Monday morning with the sound of the local radio station DJ talking loudly and harmoniously.

"G-o-o-o-d morning, all of you wonderful Californians! This is DJ Cool Boy with some good news for all you kids out there in radio land. All school buses in the district have been cancelled for the day, so roll back over, and drift off back to sleep. Hit the mall for some shopping or the beach to catch some waves. Once again, school buses for the entire district are c-c-c-cancelled for the day!"

The music on the radio begins to fill my room. My eyes open slowly as I rub the sleep from them, squinting at the bright morning light pouring in through my window.

The house is unusually quiet. My mom hasn't called me to wake up and get ready, and my dad isn't preparing breakfast. Still rubbing sleep from my eyes, I call out to my parents while coming down the stairs and finding an empty house. I begin searching the rooms and grow more and more worried.

Suddenly, the front door opens, and my worries are met with a startled jump from my mom. In a hurry, she walks through the front door with grocery bags and sets them down on the kitchen counter in a huff.

"What's wrong, Mom?" I ask, noticing Mom's mood is quite sour.

"Well, your father left on some business trip early this morning, and I have to go to work early and stay late because, apparently, half my office called in sick," she responds, clearly feeling overwhelmed.

"Where did Dad go?" I ask.

"He said something about going upstate on business. He said he would call later this evening," she replies, calmer now as she puts the groceries away. "I heard on the radio that buses were cancelled, but you still have to go to school, you know, Evyn. Go get ready, and I can drive you, or you can walk."

I am not happy to hear the news that I still have to go to school, despite the buses being canceled. Whether in this case it's due to a lack of drivers or a problem with the buses, hardly anyone shows up for school when the buses are canceled. As if things aren't bad enough, with my dad being away, I have to go to school, against my better judgment but because my mom insisted. But I very much want to see Chloe, so I decide to save Mom the drive and I walk to school.

The streets are clear when I first poke my head out the front door. There are no people, no neighbors, and, thankfully, no odd men in dark suits. It's a smoggy day, the sky so thick with pollution that the sun is barely visible through the intense gray smog. This is highly unusual, as Newport is so far from the big city and so close to the ocean that polluted air is usually blown away as quickly as it can cover Newport, but not today, for some reason. Eerie gray clouds blanket the fresh air and bright blue, sun-filled sky.

Walking to school has never been like this before. It's just like out of a scary movie. Everything seems so much more vivid and detailed. The gray shades of the smog block the sun's bright rays. I pay close attention to every single detail around me, cautious of every noise and movement.

There is no sign of anybody on the walk to school. There are no neighbors taking out the garbage or walking their pets, no shop owners on Main Street starting their busy days. As I start to wonder where everyone is, I spot Chloe just up the street from school. We see each other and smile as I greet her.

"Hey, good morning!" I happily say.

"Hey, Evyn, how was the rest of your weekend?" Chloe's words are just as warm as always to me.

"Pretty good. I just hung out around the house. Were you forced to come to school today too?"

"Yeah, my parents didn't care about the buses being cancelled."

"Yeah, mine either. Just my mom, actually. My dad left early on some business trip. Didn't say exactly where he was going—just upstate."

"Really? What a coincidence. My dad left early this morning for a work trip upstate!" Chloe's response makes me curious.

"That is a coincidence," I remark curiously.

Chloe and I brush off any ideas of our parents' peculiar work trips and head off to school. We see few kids making their way onto the school grounds—no big, yellow school buses and few cars in the parking lot. The school looks as if it were still closed for the weekend.

The halls of Sir Arthur Wilfred High School are deserted. The normal stampede of students has dwindled to a few scattered individuals. Some take to the library to study and finish homework, while others aimlessly wander the halls, going from class to class.

Very few teachers show up. Stories spread of an illness keeping teachers sick in bed; other rumors spread about peculiar business trips and work conventions that everyone's parents have gone away for. The teachers who have shown up—the ones who haven't strangely taken ill, mysteriously gone missing, or left town on an unusual work trip—attempt to organize students into classrooms to give some regularity to the school day. One would think an epidemic was forcing more than half of the school to stay home in quarantine.

The lunchroom, usually a who's who of the student body, is now all but a ghost town. The few students who do remain, like me and some friends of mine who were also forced to find their own way to school, including Sam, talk about the weird things going on.

"My dad doesn't know anything about any teacher's convention or any strange illness going around," Sam mentions.

"Pretty much everyone I've talked to says their parents have gone on business trips or to work conventions. It all sounds too weird," I say, concerned.

"My dad should be in the science lab. Let's go see him before we take off. Maybe he's heard something," Sam replies.

Sam and I leave the nearly empty cafeteria and start off down the hall toward Sam's dad's classroom. We pass by the science class and see Sam's dad, the science teacher, looking concerned as he works on his computer. We enter the classroom.

"Already over a thousand people have gone missing since the weekend. At this rate, the entire city will be missing in less than a few days. It reminds me of this story I read several months ago ..." Mr. Desjardins is saying as we approach him. He continues to explore the Internet on his computer.

Mr. Desjardins is a great teacher at the school, popular among students and teachers alike. He is also a knowledgeable and friendly father. He always has the best advice for Sam and me and has always been my favorite parent—besides my own, of course.

Mr. Desjardins goes on to show us some similar and bizarre stories on the Internet of small towns left abandoned and empty with no explanations. The stories are backed up by mysterious government agencies and men in dark suits with phony-sounding stories about chemical spills and national security issues.

Sam's dad gives a stern and frightening warning. "Whatever you do, if you notice anything strange, stay safe, and if you get any sort of bad feeling, run and hide."

The warning sticks with us as we go about our day. Coming from Sam's dad, this advice should not be taken lightly.

Sam and I go to our classes as the slow day grinds on. The empty classrooms and even emptier hallways remind me of how worried Sam's dad seemed. There is no sight of anyone anymore. It seems that everyone has decided to leave early, as there's really no point in staying at the school when it's so empty.

I stand at the school doors, looking out at the empty school grounds, curious and growing more worried about what is really going on.

"Dude, we have to go to the mall right now. Chloe and her friends are going there. She's asking about you." Sam's enthusiastic voice steals away all my concerns and he drags me out of the school with excitement.

Although the warning from Sam's dad is still fresh in my mind, the thought of spending time with the girls and my curiosity about what's really going on overwhelm me. Disregarding any concerns and parental warnings, we leave the school, venturing out into the city.

As Sam and I walk to the mall, everything looks wrong. Cars have been left abandoned; doors to houses have been left wide open; businesses along the street are closed and locked up tightly. The few shops that are open have cautious store clerks giving wary looks to anyone walking by.

Everything seems out of place. Loose house pets rummaging through garbage left by the curb, cars left running with no drivers in sight, and as we approach the mall we see abandoned cars, shopping carts and groceries littering the parking lot. Now more than ever, as Sam and I cautiously approach the mall, it becomes apparent that people have not just been going on trips or getting sick, but they have been disappearing and possibly abducted. We realize that the warning we received from Sam's dad should be taken very seriously.

We swing the large glass doors of the shopping mall open. Not a soul is in sight. When we walk in, the scene is completely different from the usual bustle of busy shoppers. It has been completely deserted, and it looks very messy, as if looters have come and gone. There are broken windows, doors left open, and stores emptied of all their goods. The whole place looks ransacked, but we put our concerns aside when we hear people in the distance. It isn't until we walk up the out-of-order escalator to the third level and around the corner to the food court that our worry turns to excitement.

Chloe and a few of her friends are hanging out in the food court, laughing over the abundance of food they have in front of them.

"Hey, guys!" Chloe happily calls out to Sam and me before pointing to her friend, Jennie, sitting beside her. "Jennie was the only person working in the mall today, and she gave us everything we wanted."

"Where is everybody?" I ask.

"Who knows?" Jennie says. "My boss said I didn't have to come in, but I need the money." Jennie's vague answer doesn't really solve anything; Sam and I join Jennie and Chloe over the feast of fast food laid out on the table, anyway.

"This place is almost as empty as school was!" Sam exclaims.

"Did you guys notice anything really weird on the way over here?" I ask.

"We drove here straight from school. We didn't really see anything at all," Chloe responds.

"That's what I mean. It's like everybody's gone—like they all left the city or something," I state inquisitively.

"Well, I, for one, think we should take advantage of the freedom," Sam declares as he hops up onto the table next to everyone, scouts out a few open doors around the food court, and comes up with some wonderful ideas. "How about we fire up the roller coaster or go play all the games in the arcade? No lineups," he says.

"I'll hang out with you guys for a bit. I've got nothing else to do." Chloe hides it well, but I'm sure she is excited to spend time with me.

CHAPTER 4

RUN!

As Chloe's best friend, Jennie, and the few other girls who have been hanging out leave to go home before it gets too late, Sam, Chloe, and I decide to venture into the empty movie theater, where there are no lines, no ticket vendors, and not a single person to interrupt our moviegoing experience.

We three adventurous teens enter the abandoned theater. The large space, normally full of long lines and crowded with patrons, now seems like a private playground set up just for Chloe, Sam, and me and our fun. With all the open space, entertaining movies, and lavish red carpeting, we have never felt such freedom as we do now. We wearily approach the snack counter on our way into the theater. The empty lobby is quite odd, and we can't help but feel a sense of daring adventure. It's not every day that such strange things occur in Newport, let alone on such a grand scale. With no one around to serve us, Sam gets the daring idea to hop over the counter, where he pretends to be a theater employee.

"Well, hello there, you beautiful young people. How can I help you? What can I get you from the wonderful snack counter?" Sam asks with a laugh. He reaches into the display shelf and grabs handfuls of all sorts of boxes of candy—chocolate-covered caramels, gummy bears, spicy, red-hot candies, and peanuts—which he tosses onto the counter for Chloe and me.

"I'm not sure if this is okay, you guys," Chloe hesitantly says.

"No one's around, Chloe. It's fine," I say confidently as I pocket a few packs of my favorite candy.

"Yeah, Chloe, no one will ever know," Sam adds as he hops back over the snack counter and joins us.

Chloe reluctantly takes a single pack of her favorite: Junior Mints. The three of us then make our way down the red-carpeted hallway of the theater lined with cinemas. We walk through a large doorway into the first large theater; the room is dark and empty.

"You guys, go get the best seats in the house. I'll go figure out how to turn on the projector and pick the best new movie I can find!" Sam excitedly states as we walk into the abandoned theater.

Chloe and I sit waiting in the darkness of the theater. We feel such a sense of freedom. All our concerns about what may be going on out in the world are drowned out as we are about to enjoy the newest blockbuster film the theater has.

"Isn't this great? We've got the whole theater to ourselves!" I exclaim, unable to hold back my excitement.

"Yeah, it's pretty awesome. I've never had an entire theater to myself. I wonder where everyone is?" Chloe asks, sitting beside me. She pulls me a little closer, seemingly worried in the darkness.

"I'm sure we'll find out soon. It's not the end of the world or anything," I say, and it calms Chloe down a bit, but then I wonder, *What if that is what's happening?*

Chloe and I get closer and closer while talking and are about to share our second kiss when, all of a sudden, the film projector fires up. It startles us both a bit but then washes our worries away as we share a laugh at our own fears. The screen lights up, with the coming attractions appearing on the massive movie screen. Chloe and I smile as we slightly lean back into our seats.

"I guess Sam figured out how to work the machine," I state with a bashful smile.

Sam comes skipping into the theater. He looks proud of himself for figuring out the complex digital projector in the abandoned projection room. He sprawls out over three seats next to Chloe and me. He puts his legs up onto the seat in front of him as he enjoys the bountiful array of snacks he has procured from the counter. Chloe and I also stretch out and enjoy the film.

But our fun in the vacant movie theater cannot last forever. The best movie experience ever soon comes to an end. As the credits roll at the end of the film, we decide to head home. We cheerfully leave the theater, the empty shopping mall echoing with quiet music playing over the speaker system. There is not a soul in sight. Everything remains odd and mysterious, and we are having too much fun to notice what's up ahead, until it's almost too late.

This can't be good, I think. "Uh, you guys, I don't mean to scare you, but I think those guys in dark suits are bad news and we should maybe get out of here," I alert my friends.

A few men in dark suits, large hats, and dark sunglasses appear at the other end of the empty shopping mall. They lock eyes with Sam, Chloe, and me and begin heading toward us, instantly followed by a loud, odd-sounding bellow from the men, which startles each of us.

"Hey, you! Stop!" One of the mysterious men in dark suits yells out.

Very determined, the men in dark suits begin their chase, and we take off running. We run through the mall as fast as we can. Our legs and feet burn beneath us as we try to outrun our mysterious pursuers. Bobbing and weaving, Sam, Chloe, and I can see no easy escape from the men, who are quickly closing in on us. The fear and tension in each of us rises, and panic sets in. Our imaginations run wild at the thought of the unforeseeable fate that may await us if these odd men should capture us.

"Why are we running?" Chloe curiously asks.

"I don't want to get in trouble for anything," Sam says as we run along the long, empty floors of the mall.

"Your dad did say to run if anything weird happened. Everything today's been pretty weird," I add as I try to keep up.

Suddenly, amid the noises of echoing footsteps, and the annoying shopping melody someone forgot to turn off, I can hear the ding of an arriving elevator just up ahead. Out of the corner of my eye, I spot the elevator door sliding open, just a few stores in front of us. While running with Chloe and Sam, I look back to see the men pursuing us are still several stores back down the mall floor. I quickly alert my friends and take Chloe by the hand, leading her to the safety of the elevator.

Sam has a quick thought and acts on it, without hesitation. "You two, go. I'm a lot faster than you guys. I'll lead them away."

Sam gets a burst of energy and quickens his speed as he keeps running, looking back to see if the men are continuing to follow him, but they have vanished.

Sam, still up on the third floor, can see the trouble his friends are about to get in on the first floor, coming off the elevator. As the doors slide open, Chloe and I come face-to-face with two men in dark suits. *How did those men get down there so fast?* Sam thinks to himself as he makes his way toward the large flight of stairs leading to the second floor.

The men and their ghostly white faces—hidden behind black sunglasses and shadowed beneath large, brimmed hats—not only frighten Chloe but also block our escape from the elevator. Chloe lets out a startling scream as the elevator doors slide open.

I fight the fear that holds me frozen, and I leap into action. Leading Chloe by the arm, I drop my shoulder low and shove myself straight into the stomach of one of the men, giving us the instant we need to sneak by and take off running once again.

One of the men behind us reaches out and grabs me tightly by the collar of my jacket, pulling me back and dropping me on the floor with a thump. *"Run, Chloe, get out of here!"* I yell.

Chloe runs but a few steps away. For a second, she looks back to see me wrestling to get free from the man, and just as she turns again and starts to run, two more men in dark suits stand right in front of her. Chloe abruptly bounces off of them, falling to the floor. One of the men grabs Chloe and starts walking, leading her by the wrist. She tries to pull free, but the man's grip is iron tight. With all her might, she wrestles to free herself but cannot budge the man's hold one bit.

Farther back down the hall, I fight with all my might to break free of the man holding me. Pulling this way and that, I tug to find release. Struggling to get free, I end up dragging the man along with me in a scuffle. I reach out and grab hold of nearby construction scaffolding. With the man forcefully pulling on my arm, I pull on the metal structure with all my might in a last-ditch effort, not really thinking of the outcome. It comes crashing down on both of us in a dusty, heaping mess of twisted metal. The crashing noise of the clanging metal pipes echoes loudly all over the quiet shopping mall.

The man in the dark suit vanishes in the colossal mess, leaving nothing but a pile of empty clothes behind. I look up for just an instant to see a heavy metal grate come swinging down toward my head. With no time to react and avoid the impact, I get knocked out cold.

Why does this stuff always happen to me? I say to myself when I wake up.

The men's pale and emotionless faces, their eyes hidden behind black sunglasses, make Chloe too scared to say a single word. The men do not speak either. Not once do they bark orders at Chloe to move; nor do they communicate with each other.

Chloe looks back and makes a fleeting split second of distressing eye contact with me. Before getting dragged out of sight, she can see me wrestling with the man just as the clanging noise of the jumbled metal pipes crashing down sounds. She can see Sam up on the second floor looking down, running to my aid while I lay unconscious under the dusty pile of fallen scaffolding.

As Chloe is dragged off to the other side of the shopping mall, more men in dark suits appear out of nowhere. They come from around corners, up staircases, and through store doorways. They all head toward Sam and me on the other side of the mall. Chloe lets out her last word to her friends in the form of a blood-curdling scream: "Run!"

Sam hears the echo of Chloe's scream from across the mall and runs for the flight of stairs leading down to the main floor. The scream wakes me up, still groggy and unaware of all that has happened. I slowly stumble to my feet, brushing the dust and debris off my clothes. I look up, dizzy, to see Sam violently leaping down the nearby flight of stairs and bounding quickly toward me. Sam comes running, having witnessed everything.

"What happened?" I ask, confused, as I shake the dizziness from my head and limp away from the mess of twisted metal scaffolding to take a seat and gather my wits.

In a completely panicked state—something I have never seen from him—Sam comes running up to me, shouting in hysterics. "Are you okay?" he says.

"Yeah, I think so," I reply, still shaken up and unaware of what exactly is going on.

"They took her! They took Chloe! Come on; we've got to save her!" Sam scoops me up by the arm while still running, helping me to my feet and almost dragging me along.

Faster and faster, Sam and I run, panicking and worried about Chloe and these strange men in dark suits. As we run through the mall, passing empty shops and deserted stores, I frantically ask Sam, "What happened?"

"They grabbed Chloe while you fought with one of them. I didn't know you had it in you. You trashed the construction pipes on one of them and got knocked out. They took her this way. I think we can catch them if we hurry," Sam explains as we continue to run.

But just then, we round a corner and stop dead in our tracks. Dozens upon dozens of men in dark suits fill the shopping mall, and we fall back over ourselves, tripping to turn and run; "fight or flight" is putting it lightly. Sam and I turn on our heels and keep running, with no escape in sight.

As the adrenaline brought on by the fear of being chased wears off, Chloe's wrist begins to hurt from the man's tight grip as they lead her through the shopping mall. Eventually, through an employees-only door, they lead her into the employee-access hallway, which surrounds the mall. The metal doors swing open with a heavy thrust on the push handles as the two men in dark suits hurry Chloe along.

The dim hallway is lit up by emergency lights along the ceiling. It takes a few disorienting moments of seeing black spots for Chloe to adjust her eyes from the bright sunlight filling the shopping mall. Now, being led through the mall's employee-access hallway, Chloe feels scared.

For several hundred steps along the dark concrete hallway, not saying a word, quickly and robotically moving forward, the men continue to march along. One of the men keeps a firm grip on Chloe's wrist, dragging her along with ease. Chloe notices they are not even looking at her. As if concentrating on something more important, they walk determinedly, focusing on something unseen ahead of them.

Chloe thinks fast and uses this to her advantage. She quickly pulls her cell phone out of her pocket with her free hand and carefully calls me, making sure not to let the men see. Finally, going around a corner and marching down a flight of stairs, the men in dark suits lead Chloe into the mall basement. They reach a dark corridor and a large door. The dismal hallway lights are broken up by a light coming from behind the large door. Rays of blue, purple, green, and orange light flicker and shoot out around all the edges of the door. As the men push the doors open, light floods out and surrounds them. Chloe gets engulfed in a brilliant spectrum of colorful, blinding light.

Unable to penetrate the dazzling array of lights, Chloe is blinded in the haze but can feel the cold grip on her wrist and the men still pulling her along until she feels faint, weak, and dizzy and can't fight the urge to fall asleep.

CHAPTER 5

KEEP RUNNING!

The mall has become a nightmare. The once-blissful shopping center is now a hunting ground in which Sam and I are the hunted. We run for our lives, like mice trapped in a maze, being chased by a ferocious pack of wildcats, our hearts beating so fast that it becomes painful.

We dart this way and that, around corners and across the shopping-mall floor. We run into a department store as fast as we can, looking for a hiding place—maybe a back exit or another way to escape. The ruthless men in dark suits are everywhere, and they are unrelenting.

Sam and I finally stop for a moment, hiding in the department store, panting and gasping for air as we crouch behind a counter.

"What is going on?" I can barely muster the strength to say the words, completely out of breath from all the running.

"I have no idea, but those guys are everywhere. Where did they all come from?" Sam blurts out, also trying to catch his breath.

"We have to find Chloe!" I say, with panic in my voice.

"How are we going to get past all of them? We can't save Chloe if we can't even save ourselves," Sam responds, looking very scared.

Suddenly, we hear the loud thumping of heavy footsteps go thundering by. Sam and I quickly go silent, holding our breath as if our lives depend on it. After a moment, Sam pokes his head up over the counter to see several of the men in suits running through the large department store. Looking out into the shopping mall, Sam can see the men running in every direction, searching for us. He drops back down behind the counter in the store and looks over to me sitting, frozen in anticipation.

"I think we lost them. We have to get out of here and come up with some kind of plan," Sam states matter-of-factly.

"Yeah, okay, let's go outside, and if we get separated, we will meet up back at my house," I respond in a whisper.

Just then, Sam and I both get startled by the loud ring of my cell phone inside my pocket, breaking the unnerving silence. Not wanting the men in suits to discover us, I quickly answer it.

"It's Chloe," I excitedly tell Sam. "Chloe, where are you?" I ask, concerned. In her quietest whisper, I am barely able to hear her, but Chloe responds.

"I'm still here at the mall. They're taking me toward the loading docks in the basement. Evyn, I'm really scared."

"Don't worry, Chloe. We're coming to get you as soon as we can."

Chloe seems reassured by my words. I fear the worst and am very worried for Chloe, but I know Sam and I must escape first, find out what's going on, and come up with a plan.

"Are you okay, Chloe?" I ask, hoping the strange men in suits have not harmed her. There is no response.

"Chloe? Chloe!" I call out louder and louder, but she is gone. I stare at my cell phone in disbelief. Anger and concern begin to overwhelm me, but thankfully, Sam draws me back to reality.

"Come on, Evyn. There's nothing we can do right now. We have to go," he says.

Sam and I cautiously sneak toward the front of the department store, watching closely for the men in dark suits who lurk everywhere. It feels as though hours pass before the coast is clear, but Sam and I eventually make a break for it.

We run from the department store and across the empty shopping mall to take cover inside a small boutique, just opposite a small mall exit. We look in all directions and quickly duck behind a counter as a group of men in suits run by on the second floor. The men pass without noticing Sam or me, so we are quickly off and running again.

As we finally make our escape from the mall, we feel the cool night air on our faces. It feels like freedom as we rush out of the mall. Suddenly, and without warning, as we turn a corner headed for the parking lot, I get grabbed by one of the men in dark suits just a few steps ahead of Sam.

Leaping into danger, without hesitation, Sam boldly runs at full speed and jumps to tackle my captor. With a loud thump, Sam rolls to the ground in an empty mess of dark clothes. He climbs to his feet through the clothes: a black suit, a dark slate overcoat, a large brimmed hat, and black sunglasses. The man has vanished.

"Did you see that guy disappear? What was that?" I ask Sam.

"I've never seen anything like it before. Like something out of a movie, he just left a pile of clothes behind!"

Puzzled by the pile of clothes, Sam and I both feel a sense of victory, but the feeling is short-lived. Just a few steps away, the mall doors slowly open, and men in dark suits pour out. An endless stream of men funnels out of the mall, and they slowly advance toward Sam and me. Like a river splitting ways, we back away in either direction, divided by the sheer number of men reaching for us. Sam and I trip over ourselves to get our feet under us, and once again, we are off and running.

"Go, Evyn, run!" Sam cries out as he takes off running from the shopping mall.

"Meet at my place!" I reply as I also set off running, in the opposite direction through the parking lot.

I quickly hide in the parking lot and lose the men in dark suits as they continue running. I dart quickly around a corner and hop into an abandoned car to wait patiently as the strange men go running by. After some time passes, I cautiously look in all directions through the car's windows, and then slowly, I creep out of the car.

Then I begin the long and treacherous journey home. The streets have never before been so quiet or seemed so long in my neighborhood. The grief caused by letting Chloe get taken by the men in suits and the uncertainty of what will become of her and Sam weigh heavily on my mind. I have never before felt quite as alone as I do slowly making my way home.

Sneaking from one building to the next to avoid being discovered, I desperately try to get home and meet up with Sam. Scared that Sam may have also been captured by these mysterious men in suits, I can hardly bear the thought, so I try to focus on getting home, safe and sound.

Just when I thought things couldn't get any worse, I say to myself.

As I cautiously poke my head out of an alleyway and around a corner on Main Street, someone throws a large rock through a nearby shop window, shattering it to pieces. I was not expecting this. A large group of men rushes into the shop and begins stealing everything they can get their hands on. I get down in the alley and lean against a brick wall.

I am not as scared as I am shocked by what could become of Newport if nobody figures out how to stop what's going on. *What do these mysterious men want? What will become of the city if no one stops this invasion? Is it just Newport that's being taken over? Where did these awful men come from, and why are they even interested in Newport? Where are the police in all of this? Why aren't they stopping it?*

I am not sure of anything anymore. I'm so overwhelmed by questions and worry, but in a single sweep, I brush my worries off, putting my concerns aside, as I sense my life may soon be in danger yet again.

The noises from the looters smashing the window draws the men in dark suits' attention. The last of the looters, leaping through the broken shop window and into the street, runs off with stolen merchandise.

As the looter runs by, I duck back deeper into the alley, into the shadows of an alcove. I can hear footsteps approaching faster and louder. I recognize the sound of shoes, and I know what is coming. A moment later, dozens of men in matching dark suits go running by.

As the men in dark suits run right by me on the street, without even glancing down the alley in my direction, I hold my breath in hopes that they won't notice me. Once they've past, I let out the breath I was holding in my lungs and take a few big breaths. I believe holding my breath may have helped, but I know I just got lucky. I wait for just a moment around the corner until, eventually, I slowly get to my feet. Peeking out around the corner of the building once again, I look carefully in all directions. I look up and down Main Street, across the street, into a parking lot, in every corner, and in each nook and cranny. The scene is wild.

Groups of men in dark suits and black sunglasses are everywhere. They chase the looters, who have split up in an effort to confuse the men in suits. Some of the looters try to fight off the men in dark suits but with no hope. The men in dark suits simply outnumber the looters, and one after another, all the looters are captured and taken away in a large black van.

I feel much more scared now and alone. I slip back down the alley as shock sets in, and I wait for what feels like an instant, but almost an hour goes by before I finally look around the corner again. The coast is clear, for now.

Sam runs from the shopping mall and heads toward downtown. After he's separated from me, he runs as fast as he can in the only direction available. Being chased by a large group of men in dark suits, I can only watch for a moment as I run in the opposite direction.

Sam sees me in the distance through the mall parking lot, running toward Main Street and being chased by another huge crowd of men in dark suits. He quickly rounds the first corner of buildings away from the mall and instantly ducks into an office building. He sprints through the empty lobby and up a flight of stairs. He bursts through the first open door he can find and carefully looks out a window, so as not to be seen. Scared and gasping for breath, he looks outside, down toward the street, worrying about his friends. Sam feels totally overwhelmed by the fear and uncertainty caused by all that has happened and what may happen, if he should get captured.

The men in dark suits flood out around the corner and down onto the street. Sam's heart sinks into his belly as the men slow down. They linger for a moment, looking in all directions, up and down the streets, pacing in an odd formation. Sam slinks back to avoid being seen and notices a bizarre similarity among the men in suits. Every single one of them appears to wear the same dark suit, large hat, and black sunglasses. Their faces all look pale, hidden in the shadows of their hats, but Sam brushes it off, thinking the clothes and glasses must be government issued. Before circling back toward the shopping mall, the men all look at each other, not saying a word. Sam finds it peculiar, as if they are somehow communicating with each other without speaking.

Sam's fear completely overrides his curious concern as he waits there, in the office. For what feels like a few hours, he tries to gather his thoughts and brush off his fears. Eventually, he makes the brave decision to venture out into the world. He peers out the window once again to make sure the coast is clear on the street before heading back into the city toward Main Street.

Easily avoiding detection, like a small animal in the city streets, Sam moves from one building to the next, down alleyways and backstreets, as he makes his way to my house. Eventually, Sam makes it to the large, open field, separating the large buildings of downtown Newport from the smaller businesses and houses of the suburban neighborhoods near Main Street. Students travel through this clearing every day to get to and from school, but not today. The men in dark suits are everywhere, walking around like guard dogs, patrolling the streets.

Hidden from sight, behind the corner of a back alley, Sam watches out over the open expanse and waits cautiously as he thinks up a plan to evade the men and reach the safety of the suburbs. *If I can just make it to the houses, I could lose them,* Sam thinks to himself as he continues to spy on the men in suits from the safety of the dense buildings that divide downtown and Main Street.

Suddenly, in the distance, Sam hears a loud, resounding *crash* of shattering glass. Looters have thrown a rock through a shop window on Main Street. The men in dark suits instantly turn their heads and run off toward the loud noise of the broken window. Sam sees his opening and, without hesitation, takes the opportunity.

There is a gap between the men now, large enough for Sam to quickly run from his vantage point, go across the field, and duck behind a small group of bushes at the back of the shops on Main Street. The men do not notice him, as they have gone to investigate the smashed glass farther up Main Street, but as Sam peaks over the shrubs, a lone man in a dark suit spots him. All of a sudden, several men chase after him again.

Sam darts as quickly as he can from the small outcropping of bushes to the closest house he can see. The fence surrounding the house is high, but Sam's body races with adrenaline, so he scampers up the fence, scratching his leg as he flops over the top of it. He lands with a *thump* on the other side of the fence and limps to his feet.

He brushes off the dirt and examines the small scrapes on his leg as he hobbles toward the house. He bangs on the back door as he opens it, yelling as he enters, "Hello! Is anybody home?"

There is no answer, but Sam hasn't got time to worry about the consequences of breaking in. He grabs a shirt from a laundry pile inside the house as he makes his way to the front door. He tightly wraps the shirt over the scrapes on his leg and ties it off. Carefully, he spies out the front window of the house. He waits until there has been no sign of anyone for several minutes and then makes a break for the next house, then the next house, and the next. Cautiously watching for the men, Sam waits for quite a while at every house to make sure the area is clear before darting to the next house.

Not until Sam almost arrives at my house does trouble find him. Into the homestretch, feeling as lucky as a lottery winner to have made it this far safely, Sam grows careless with his strategy. He continues his stealthy walk, sneaking quickly and quietly behind another house. In the backyard, he keeps a lookout for any sign of trouble as he makes his way over a fence. With his injured leg, he slowly makes the climb and carefully descends on the other side.

As Sam continues, he forgets to look out for anything besides men in dark suits. Over another fence, he drops to his feet, landing with a thump. As he lifts his head, he is greeted by a deep, snarling growl. Sam is frozen in fear; the last thing he expected to encounter were hungry, abandoned house pets. Two mean, overprotective, and very large dogs bear down on him with teeth snarling as they bark and run. Sam does the only thing his body will allow him to do: with all the energy he has left, Sam runs for his life.

CHAPTER 6

RESCUE PLAN

I wait at my house, pacing back and forth between the kitchen and the living room. I carefully watch out the windows of the front and back of the house, hoping to see Sam any second now.

Come on, where are you, Sam? I anxiously think, hoping, more than ever, to see Sam come running through the backyard.

The sun begins to set slowly over the horizon, streaming a vibrant cascade of brilliant oranges and reds across the sky. Finally, as the sun is just about to set over the towering buildings of downtown and the hills beyond that, I see Sam pop out across the street. Sam runs as fast as he can through the yards, chased by two mean, barking dogs.

I frantically bolt into action, swinging the back door open while yelling for Sam to hurry up and get inside. Sam quickly rounds the corner of the house and jumps through the open door as I slam it shut behind him.

"Those dogs are making way too much noise!" I exclaim, worried they will attract the unwanted attention of the mysterious men in suits.

"Trust me. I didn't plan on them chasing me!" Sam says, catching his breath as I continue to speak.

"Are you okay? I thought for sure they caught you."

"Yeah, I'm fine. I cut my leg, but I'll live. I had a few close calls. What about you?" Sam asks.

"Same thing; it's crazy out there. But I'm all right. Come on. There's a first aid kit in the washroom. We've got to hide. Follow me." I lead the way upstairs to the pull-down staircase that goes to the attic. With the first aid kit in hand, I pull the cord, and the stairs slide down for us to climb to hiding.

My attic is dusty and dark, with just one small window overlooking the front of the house. It has lots of storage, dusty boxes, and a large, comfy area, which I set up for privacy ages ago. There's a small desk with an old television and a lamp on it. Sleeping bags, from when I felt like camping in the attic when I was younger, lie collected in a corner. For many nights, the attic was my getaway place when I felt like being alone.

"Here, you're going to want to spray some of this on your cut and then wrap it up," I say as I pass Sam a bottle of disinfectant and some gauze from the first aid kit. Then I change the subject. "I'm so worried about Chloe. How are we going to save her? How are we even going to find her?" I ask as I persistently try to call her on my cell phone.

"I'm sure she's fine. I don't think these crazy guys in suits are killing anyone," Sam replies, seemingly trying to relieve some of my stress.

"Come on, Chloe. Where are you? She's not answering." I continue calling Chloe, but there is no response.

"I've been trying my dad too. He's not answering either. What about your folks?" Sam asks.

"They haven't been around since yesterday. I swear, this is some kind of secret invasion," I declare, overwhelmed and frightened.

"What do you mean? Like aliens or something?" Sam questions, puzzled.

"No, but maybe some kind of secret government cover-up, like what your dad told us about." My answer seems to sound reasonable to Sam.

"Well, we've done everything we can do for now. Let's just get some sleep, and we can try to figure things out tomorrow," Sam suggests, exhausted.

Sam and I quickly grow tired of sitting in the attic. As the night drags on, Chloe's absence and our parents' unknown whereabouts take their toll. All our unanswered questions and the threatening men in suits' looming presence leave Sam and me with a never-before-experienced sensation of fear. Hope diminishes as we sit in my attic, becoming more worried, not only scared for our loved ones but also overwhelmed by the problems we must deal with.

We eventually decide to go to sleep in order to get a fresh start in the morning. All of the running and our new, overwhelming fears—all of the unanswered questions—have left both Sam and I extremely tired.

I try to sleep. I try to forget the horrible things that have happened in the last twenty-four hours and the daunting tasks that lie ahead. I try so hard to just clear my mind and fall asleep—and try even harder to ignore the sounds of Sam snoring next to me. But, despite my efforts, I am unable to sleep a wink. All I can think about is getting to Chloe. The guilt of losing her in the mall hangs over me like a dark cloud.

We must get to her before it's too late; we have to get to her in time. Thoughts keep racing in my mind; over and over, I play out multiple scenarios in my head. *What horrible things are the sinister men in dark suits doing to her? What must she be going through, and is she still alive? Even if she did manage to get free of the men, she must be all alone and scared, trying to escape the shopping mall, which is littered with the scary men in suits. What if they have her caged up, like some sort of wild animal, or they're torturing her with all kinds of diabolical devices?*

More than anything, I hope that Chloe is safe and unharmed.

If this is the case, I am confident that I can rescue her, and then I'll know that she is all right.

Finally, fed up with my torturous thoughts, I roll over to face Sam, who is fast asleep beside me on the attic floor.

"Sam. Hey, Sam, are you awake?" I ask, already knowing I am waking Sam up with the question. There is a brief silence.

"No, Ev, I'm asleep," Sam replies sarcastically, with his eyes still closed.

"What are we going to do? We need to come up with a plan," I say quietly and with concern.

"In the morning, Evyn; go back to sleep," Sam responds, exhausted, and instantly falls asleep.

A long moment of silence passes as I sit awake, wondering how Sam can sleep at a time like this. So much has happened, and so many questions remain unanswered. Finally, I lay my head down and somehow manage to doze off.

Sam and I wake up to sunlight streaming in through the small attic window. The bright morning light breaks the attic's darkness and brightens up the large, dusty space. Sam and I both needed that sleep. We needed the energy to recover after all the running we did, and we need that energy to face the daunting tasks that lie ahead of us.

We slowly sit up on our sleeping bags, rubbing the sleep from our eyes. We quickly try to form a plan. As futile as it seems, we feel better knowing we have some sort of strategy in an otherwise-hopeless mission.

"Okay, so first we have to get back to the shopping mall safely." Sam makes the first contribution to the plan.

"We'll also need some kind of diversion to distract the men in suits so we can get inside. I think I have an idea for that." I add my portion of the plan, thinking about several action movies I have recently watched. Movie heroes always come up with the most outrageous plans—plans that would ordinarily never work out but that somehow go off without a hitch.

"So we make the diversion, and we sneak into the mall. Hopefully, we find Chloe somewhere in the basement and get out of the mall without getting caught," I say. Sam shakes his head in disbelief to the plan. "I know it sounds impossible, Sam, but what else can we do?" I plead with him.

"I know, Ev; you're right. It's just that we don't know anything about these guys in suits. There's something seriously scary about them. How are we going to rescue Chloe? What can we possibly do to stop so many of these guys?" Sam speaks plainly and realistically.

"We will have to do our best to sneak in, maybe through an air vent or something. There are big air-conditioning pipes in the underground parking lot." I try to hide my desperation as I continue. "Maybe we can sneak in through those and find Chloe without even being seen."

"Let's just get going. We'll figure it out when we get there, if we even make it to the shopping mall …" Sam hopelessly states as he lifts the attic staircase rope, letting down the steps.

We grab a few supplies from the kitchen, like some school snacks from the cupboard and some bottles of water from the fridge, and make our way into the garage. Surveying its collection of tools and odds and ends, Sam and I put a couple of large pry bars into our backpacks before we cautiously exit the house. We are wary yet confident in our plan to rescue Chloe.

The streets are deserted; there is not a soul in sight. Newport is a mess. We see broken house windows, doors left open, and abandoned cars lining the streets. Even the house pets, whose owners have seemingly vanished, have abandoned the streets for somewhere safer.

The shops appear to be in shambles as we make our way up Main Street and into the dense, tall buildings of downtown Newport. There are broken-in doors and smashed windows everywhere. Sam and I do not see or hear much of anything on the trek through downtown. No cars drive through the streets, no people gather anywhere, and all the businesses still remain closed. Even the usual, quiet chirps of birds and the rustling of trees are absent.

After hours of sneaking through downtown Newport, along its concrete alleyways and open streets, Sam and I slowly approach our last corner. From the safety of a back alleyway, we spot the last stretch of road leading to the shopping mall. Then Sam and I poke our heads out around the corner of the building and see the immense Fashion Island Mall in the distance. Our hearts sink into our bellies when we see that the mall is completely surrounded by the men in dark suits.

"Okay, so what's the big diversion you have in mind?" Sam asks me as we hopelessly watch the army of men in dark suits blocking our path.

"We need to find a car that's been abandoned but still has the keys in it," I answer, knowing full well there are plenty of abandoned cars throughout the city.

It doesn't take long for us to find a car with the keys in it. I grab a small stick from a nearby alley and explain to Sam what he has to do. "We need to get as close to the mall as possible without being seen. You're going to jam the gas pedal so the car will drive off and lead the men away from the mall. Once we get our opening, we will run for the underground parking lot."

"You know this is crazy, right? Let's just say we *do* make it to the underground parking lot. What will stop the men from seeing us and just grabbing us, like they have done with everyone else?" Sam doubtfully asks.

"We're going to hop into the vent shafts as fast as we can. The men are too big to look for us in there," I masterfully remark as my courage grows.

"I think you've seen too many spy movies, but it just might work." Sam accepts the proposed plan.

Up the street from the mall, Sam slowly drives the car from its roadside, parked position and lines it up with the shopping-mall parking lot.

"Once I let this thing go, there's no telling where it will end up," Sam declares, hoping for a successful result.

"After the car gets going, we will need to sneak up quickly and get to the underground parking lot as fast as we can." My vague reply shows my uncertainty of the plan.

Sam pauses, sitting in the driver's seat with the car idling, thinking about how best to set the lone car off and running on its own. He takes a deep breath and readies himself for what's about to happen. With one foot on the break, Sam shifts the car into neutral and pushes the stick down against the gas pedal. The engine kicks in and rumbles. The noise is enough to get the men in suits' attention. After a split second, Sam pulls the gear shift into drive and jumps out of the car. The car then goes flying off toward the shopping mall and the unsuspecting men in dark suits.

Sam and I begin our strategic approach to the mall. We can see the car spinning off in the opposite direction, toward the far side of the mall. The men in dark suits turn to look at the fast-approaching vehicle and give chase, leaving a small opening for us to run safely to the hidden maze of the underground parking lot.

The car hits a curb. It goes flying up into the air and rushes into a cloud of dust, making a sharp left turn upon landing and heading back toward the parking lot. Now on a collision course with the runaway car, they must quickly jump out of the way to avoid it. The car races toward the men in dark suits, who easily dodge it before it crashes into the concrete walls of the shopping mall.

Curiously enough, the men quickly lose interest in the wrecked car and turn back toward the parking lot and the shopping-mall entrance. Our distraction works perfectly, but we have to move quickly, as we are running out of time.

Just in time, as the men turn their gaze back our direction, we run briskly through the underground parking lot and round a corner, coming face-to-face with a large metal vent. As we run, we swiftly pull out the pry bars we took from my house and we start prying at the metal clasps that hold it in place. We unlock the two bottom clasps just enough to pry open the heavy grate and sneak through into the dusty metal shafts.

"I can't believe that worked," Sam whispers as he gasps to catch his breath.

"Yeah, no kidding, that was awesome!" I reply, equally out of breath from running and struggling with the vent cover.

"Now what do we do?" Sam asks with uncertainty.

Sam and I find ourselves at the start of a dark, dusty metal shaft. The air-conditioning system is a never-ending maze of tight tunnels, which goes through the entire shopping mall. The long, narrow shafts offer no room for Sam and me, just enough to squeeze through and crawl along slowly, with no real idea of where we are or where we're going.

Carefully avoiding the holes that drop through to the lower levels of the shopping malls venting system, and being extra careful at loose points where the weak metal shafts bend and give way, we make our way toward a small, bright light down the shaft. With nothing but a dim cell-phone light leading the way, Sam and I find ourselves in near darkness.

We ultimately arrive at another large vent. In front of me, Sam can see the concrete floor and brick walls of the basement on the other side. He does not see anyone in the basement hallway, so he begins trying to pry the vent open. He thrusts and pushes with all his might in order to loosen it enough to crawl out, but it doesn't work. He eventually gives up and turns around in the narrow shaft in hopes that he can use his legs to break through the vent.

Then Sam is able to kick out the vent. It falls to the floor below with a clattering bang. We wait for a moment, worried about attracting the men in suits' unwanted attention.

"You think they heard that?" Sam curiously asks me.

"Let's hope not."

We hurriedly jump down from the dirty ventilation shaft and run for cover in a nearby supply closet.

"Where do we start looking?" Sam asks.

"Chloe mentioned they were leading her toward the loading docks of the mall. They're around the far-back side, where all the big delivery doors are. I think it's that way," I respond, pointing down the hallway.

CHAPTER 7

ESCAPE PLAN

Sam and I finally make it to the shopping-mall warehouse. All the shopping-mall stores and businesses get their products here. From outside, huge garage doors open up to a massive loading bay. The basement warehouse is usually stocked with supplies and merchandise waiting to go into the stores. All the way to the ceiling on the enormous shelves and as far as the eye can see, merchandise stretches out along the warehouse floor.

We quietly enter through the large double doors from the basement hallway and freeze in shock and awe at the most unexpected, incredible sight: the storage warehouse, stretching out for the entire length of the mall, is entirely filled with people. Thousands of townspeople lay row after row on small tables, while others stand silent and motionless in a zombielike trance, crowded into the immense room. Young and old people lay unconscious and plugged into a weird array of wires and glowing tubes, all of which lead to another room.

"Oh my God," Sam whispers, in shock.

"The entire city must be in here," I remark, astounded by this incredible sight.

Sam investigates the large groups of people. He cannot make sense of why they are simply standing motionless, frozen in some sort of bizarre trance, with their eyes foggy and absent of color. He waves his hands in front of the people's faces, calling out to them in curiosity. "Hello? Anybody in there?" he asks them.

Like a miracle, I quickly spot Chloe close to the entrance, her long, blonde hair shimmering in the dim emergency lights of the basement warehouse. I rush over to her and quickly unplug her from the bizarre cables, pulling a wire out of her arm. I then notice a thin, clear tube pulsating from behind her ear.

As I carefully slide the electric tube out of Chloe's neck, an alarm goes off. Echoing throughout the basement, its resounding, high-pitched whine carries on beeping without end.

"That can't be good," Sam declares.

"Come on; let's hurry. Help me move her!" Frantically, I call to Sam while helping Chloe get off the table.

Sam and I each put one of Chloe's arms around our shoulders. She is barely conscious as we start off through the warehouse. Behind us, we can see men in dark suits emerging out of nowhere. Among the hundreds of rows of people lying on medical tables, the three of us struggle to make our way to the large double doors.

Reaching the doors, we quickly exit the room and stop just outside, in the corridor. Chloe, still barely able to stand, collapses in Sam's arms. Nearby is a janitors cart and I quickly get an idea. I grab a long broom and slide its long handle through the doors curved latches, jamming the doors shut behind us. Off Sam and I go, running down the concrete hallway and up the stairs, helping Chloe along with us.

Behind all the stores in the mall, hidden from what shoppers can see, we reach the employee-access hallway. A colossal maze of concrete stands behind all the mall's decoratively designed walls and appealing architecture. These tunnels and hallways connect the stores, restaurants, and storage and utility rooms, as well as the stairs and service elevators connecting all three floors of the mall and the basement. Sam, Chloe, and I find ourselves lost in the maze, our sense of direction failing us as we run for our lives.

The loud, thundering *crash* of a distant door banging open, followed by loud footsteps, echoes in the hallway behind us. The men have entered the hallway and are quickly closing in on us. As we move as quickly as possible, Sam and I frantically check every door we pass along the never-ending concrete hallway, all the while supporting poor Chloe, who is still weak and disoriented from whatever these men are doing to the townspeople.

"Are they still chasing us?" Chloe whispers as she slowly wakes up.

Our sweat and exhaustion are becoming overwhelming when we finally get a lucky break, and one of the solid metal doors opens with a twist of its handle. Sam and I quickly file through, helping Chloe in, and move from the employee-access hallway into a store.

Sam locks the door behind us as I run to the front of the bed-and-bath store to make sure the coast is clear. Luckily for us, the store's front door is locked and secured. The store offers a safe haven, even if just for a few moments.

"I'm so scared. Aren't you guys scared?" Chloe asks, breathing heavily and shaking, still frightened from being chased by the army of men in dark suits.

"We lost them, Chloe. We'll be safe in here for a while," Sam responds sternly, as if to assure himself as well as Chloe before he goes to look around the store.

"Yeah, we're fine, Chloe. As long as we keep out of sight, they won't find us in here," I say as I sit next to Chloe in the back corner of the store. I reach into my backpack and hand Chloe a bottle of water that I grabbed from my house. She instantly reaches out with both arms and pulls me close.

"Here, I found these all over the store," Sam says, walking up to Chloe and me with his arms full of plush blankets and soft pillows. "There's a lot more, and I think I saw a lunchroom. I'll go see if there is any food or more drinks."

"What was that room in the basement? What were they doing to everyone down there?" Chloe asks, concerned.

"I have no idea, Chloe, but we'll figure everything out soon enough," I answer, equally concerned about all the people hooked up to the strange tubes and wires.

Are our parents in there? Is the whole city trapped in the basement? What exactly are these men doing to everyone? Waves of unanswered questions swirl in my mind as Sam, Chloe, and I huddle together in the back of the store.

"What are we going to do?" Sam asks, after we've had a chance to gather our thoughts.

"We have to save everyone," I reply.

"But how? It was hard enough to get me out!" Chloe reminds us that we are still trapped in the mall. But there, in the bed-and-bath store, we manage to find some comfort and safety for the night.

CHAPTER 8

A HERO IS BORN

The sun can't rise fast enough. Sam, Chloe, and I have been hiding scared all night in the back of the mall's bed-and-bath store. The rising sun fills the dirty shopping mall with a dazzling light, which accents all the dust and vandalized stores of the once-prestigious and -elegant mall.

It is completely quiet in the mall when Sam and I poke our heads out to check for men in dark suits. Not a soul is in sight—no men in dark suits and no reason for us not to leave quickly.

Sam slowly and carefully opens the front door to the store and spies into the empty mall. "Okay, it's clear. Let's go. Stay quiet, and keep an eye out. Who knows if those guys are still around somewhere?" Sam says as we sneak out of the store and look for an exit.

With no sign of the men in dark suits anywhere, Sam, Chloe, and I make a stealthy exit. We are so relieved to see a way out of the shopping mall. *If I never go shopping again, it will be too soon.* We all now share a similar disgust for the mall, which has been a place fit for nightmares for the last couple of days.

We exit the mall through a side door, but at the last moment, men in suits spot us from across the mall parking lot, and like so many times before, they give chase. The group of men suddenly starts to multiply. A handful becomes a dozen, and then several dozen, until almost a hundred men are running through the parking lot after us.

Compelled by fear, we run through the parking lot. With a sea of men in dark suits chasing us, Sam, Chloe, and I know there is no way we can outrun them again. As we sneak past several abandoned cars left behind by abducted shoppers, I notice keys hanging from car doors. Through some car windows, I can even see sets of keys still in the ignitions.

"Hey, Sam, you know how to drive, right?" I quickly and desperately ask him.

Sam gets the idea right away and cracks a big smile. We all hop into an abandoned car, which fires up on the first try. Then we fly through the parking lot. Quickly rounding a corner, we stop, facing a wall of men in dark suits. Sam slams on the brakes and throws the car in reverse. Squealing the tires, Sam races us backward through a stretch of parking lot and hops a curb, flying us out into the empty street. In a mess of dust and the burning smell of rubber, the car stalls. There we sit, hopeless and stuck out in the open. Sam struggles to get the car started again.

"I thought you knew how to drive!" Chloe says in a panic.

"I never said I was good at it," Sam modestly replies.

"They're coming. Quick, let's get out of here! They're right there!" I cry out as hundreds upon hundreds of men in dark suits come flooding out of the parking lot behind us.

The car suddenly fires back to life, and we take off, swerving left and right, speeding through the empty streets. Sam barely avoids abandoned cars as the car smashes through piles of garbage on the side of the road. With Sam behind the wheel and me holding on for dear life in the passenger seat, poor Chloe sits in the backseat, getting tossed back and forth.

Men in dark suits appear on every street corner as we race

through the streets of Newport. Even hundreds more men appear everywhere, blocking off streets. Moving through the streets in our stolen getaway car, we fear there is no escape.

Not until we circle back toward the mall, with no other roads available, do I see the hopeless expressions on Chloe's and Sam's faces.

How many times will I turn and run? How many times will I not have the courage to stand up to bullies in all their forms? When you know something is wrong, when is enough, enough? I've got to do something! These thoughts reach the boiling point in my mind as we are so close to escaping these evil men in suits yet again. My feelings overwhelm me, and I just stop. I decide to take a stand. I calmly turn to Sam and plainly say, "Sam, take Chloe, and get out of here. I'm going to end this, once and for all."

"What are you talking about? You're crazy!" Sam responds, trying to reason with me.

"What can you possibly do against so many of these men?" Chloe, scared and confused, also tries to get a rational answer from me.

"I've got a plan," I respond, not really sure of what I'll do but feeling positive that doing something is better than nothing.

I fill Sam and Chloe in on my idea. "Pull up as close as you can to that air vent we snuck into earlier, and I'll hop out. Lead the men away as fast as you can. Keep driving, and try to get away. I'm going to get some answers in the mall basement."

"And then what?" Chloe asks, growing frustrated.

"Yeah, I don't know, Evyn. It was hard enough rescuing Chloe. And we haven't even gotten away yet." Sam, still driving, doesn't agree with the plan, but at least it's a plan. Suddenly, he stops the car, slamming on the brake next to the mall, leaving skid marks behind us, and he looks over at me, saying, "Stay hidden, Evyn. Run as fast as you can. I'll try to keep them busy out here. Call Chloe's phone."

I gather my wits as I hop out of the car. I run for the hidden air vent just around a corner in the underground parking lot of the mall.

Sam unwillingly leaves my side with Chloe to make their way to safety. He drives off quickly, squealing the tires as they disappear around the corner.

I am all alone now, I think, scared and more determined than ever to find answers. I climb into the hidden tunnels of the air vents. In the nearly black air shafts of the shopping mall, one arm in front of the other, I crawl through the narrow tunnel. As Sam and I did when we rescued Chloe, I make my way straight along the same path toward the light up ahead. The dusty metal passage offers no light and no room. I gradually inch along, squeezing in tightly to make my way to the basement.

As I approach the broken grate that opens up to the shopping-mall basement, I can see down into the concrete hallways through small air-vent openings. I am suddenly shocked and frightened to see dozens of men in dark suits lining the basement walls. Standing in rows along the walls, they are still and silent, as if on guard. I find it curious to see all the men standing like statues. I wonder how I will ever make it to the townspeople and somehow stop this madness before I am also caught by these mysterious men in suits.

Without warning, as I crawl through the metal vent shaft, it begins to shake. Loosened by Sam and me the last time we were here, the tunnel shifts, and I come crashing down into the hallway with a mess of dust and debris. I know this is not going well; fear sinks in, as I know the men are everywhere around me. Crawling to my feet, I am surprised to see the men standing still and silent along the walls of the basement hallway.

Confused and terrified, I don't understand what is happening. The men remain standing there in rows, in their dark suits and black sunglasses, their large hats hiding their pale faces. The ominous, statue-like men don't move a muscle or say a word. They don't give chase or even acknowledge that they see me standing there beside the dusty mess of the fallen vent shaft.

"Hello ...?" Frozen in fear, I quietly call out, but there is no response. I take a few steps and hear a strange voice behind me, sounding mysterious and almost robotic.

"We've been waiting for you."

I whip my head around, but the men in suits remain perfectly still. Confused, I pause, frightened by the sudden announcement. I wonder why the men aren't chasing me.

"Hello?" I awkwardly ask the men. Then I cautiously walk up to and poke one of the men's chest to see if he is even alive.

A second later, as I examine another man, I jump back, startled as the man quickly turns his head to me and that same deep, harmonic voice again blurts out, "We've been waiting for you, Evyn Hunter."

"How do you know my name?" I angrily call out, but there is no response. "What's going on? What are you doing here?" Growing more frustrated, I shout at the men, but again, there is no response. The men simply stand frozen, not moving a muscle and not saying a word. I start walking toward the large warehouse.

One after another, the men in dark suits call out to me as I slowly walk by.

"We've been waiting for you."

"Keep going."

"Evyn Hunter."

"We've been waiting for you."

I walk faster as the robotic voices call out to me. My fear from being chased by these strange men in dark suits is now dwarfed by the confusing and mysterious chants emanating from them. The unsettling voices echo down the concrete hallway, and I cannot help but run, surrounded by the beckoning and frightening words.

"Keep going."

"We've been waiting for you."

"Evyn Hunter."

"We've been waiting for you."

"Keep going."

"Evyn Hunter."

"Evyn Hunter."

"Evyn Hunter."

Suddenly, as I run around a corner approaching the corridor to the mall's large basement warehouse, the voices stop. I look back down the hallway and see that the dozens of men are gone. How strange it seems. *Where did they all go? What on earth is going on?* I think as I continue toward the warehouse.

I watchfully walk down the dim basement hallway toward the warehouse, where all the townspeople are being held. I am more determined than ever to face the threat—determined to get to the bottom of the evil men's plans, to get answers, and to stop them and rescue everyone.

Down the concrete corridor leading to the large warehouse, where the evil men in suits have been keeping the townspeople, I can see an array of blue and white lights shining through the door, lights that weren't there before.

What have I gotten myself into? I think as I warily approach the door.

As I open the door, I see that the large room is still filled with all the people, lying on medical tables or grouped together in large crowds, standing still and silent, with tubes and wires connected to them. Off on the far side of the large warehouse, beyond the crowds of people standing like statues in an eerie daze, I can see where the lights are coming from. Within a large room, where all the wires and tubes gather, three shadowy figures sit around an unusual machine. Three men in dark suits manipulate the large metal machine, which is taking up almost the entire room.

As I slowly move through the large warehouse of sleeping people, careful not to disturb anything, I can now see clearly the three men in dark suits working on the strange-looking machine. Slowly and courageously, I walk up behind the three men who sit with their backs turned to me. The man in the center, in a dark suit and large hat, sits focusing on a large holographic screen. The man lifts his head as I enter the room. He removes the dark, large-brimmed hat from his head, revealing a full head of long, pure-white hair. He also removes his black sunglasses and lets out a sigh of relief as he stands up from the computer and faces me. On both sides of him, the two other men also stand. They take off their large coats and black sunglasses and set them on the table. They both slowly turn toward me.

I stand frozen, not scared or threatened, but shocked to see the men's faces for the first time. Their faces are young and soft looking, not aged by time, but old and simultaneously vibrant and youthful. It is the men's eyes that shock me the most, with deep purple and blue orbs that swirl with brilliant light, moving inside their sockets with changing colors that seem to go on forever.

Then, in the most peculiar of voices, almost robotic and slightly hypnotizing, the men take turns calmly saying sentences in a harmonic and mesmerizing tone.

"We have been waiting a long time for you."

"We know who you are, Evyn Hunter."

"We have been traveling the universe since the beginning of time, and we have seen the future."

"A future including you ..."

CHAPTER 3

WE COME IN PEACE

For the first time, I realize that these are not men at all—not humans but instead some sort of alien beings. The idea takes a few moments to settle in.

This is the most unbelievable thing I have ever experienced. After collecting my thoughts and gathering my courage, I speak to the aliens. The aliens speak one after the other, as if sharing one mind. In an odd, harmonious, deep, and echoing voice, they string their sentences together.

"How do you know my name?" I curiously ask.

"We know you from our universe."

"The Evyn Hunter there is … different."

"We cannot transform him."

"We need your universe's energy to fix our machine."

This has to be some kind of hoax, I think. Their answers only bring more questions to mind. *What is this other universe, and who is this other Evyn? They want energy—what energy, how, and for what purpose?* With so many questions swirling in my head, I can only bring myself to ask these beings one thing.

"Why do you keep referring to yourself as 'we'?" I curiously muster the question, completely confused by the aliens' remarks about me: Evyn Hunter, a simple nobody from Newport. *There's nothing special about me. What could they possibly know about me?*

The three aliens continue to weirdly take turns responding.

"We are all that is left in this dimension."

"Three forms are all that remain of our entire race."

"We are one."

"We were trapped in this world."

"We mean no harm to these humans."

"It is the only way we know how to survive."

"So why don't you let everyone go?" I try to hide my anger in the demanding question.

"We must live."

"We require energy."

"We are energy."

The aliens are puzzled by and curious of my apparently absurd question, as if I should already know the answer.

I grow more curious than the aliens and ask more questions.

"How come there are so many other men in dark suits?" I ask.

"Thousands of years ago, we learned to fabricate our energy into matter."

"We are one."

"We needed to expand."

"We create helpers."

The aliens speak in turns, one after the other, as they go on explaining to me, using the most peculiar and hypnotizing voices.

"We live off the energy of other beings."

"We must live."

"We have no choice."

"We are trapped."

I start to understand that these aliens mean no harm, but rather are surviving the only way they know how. I offer them a solution.

"If you can manipulate energy, how are you trapped? Why don't you just blast off back to your planet?" I ask.

The aliens grow more frustrated—angry, even—as they lose interest in me. Two of the aliens keep talking to me while the other turns and continues to meticulously work on their unusual machine.

"We are trapped."

"Our device is malfunctioning."

"We cannot leave."

"This is now our planet."

"We must fix the device."

"With a specific human-type of energy."

"It was much easier than we expected."

"To capture and subdue the energy from these humans."

In outrage, no longer able to hold my composure, I angrily blurt out, "That's because humans are trusting. We're compassionate and loving people! You kidnapped them all, and you're torturing everyone!"

"It will be over soon."

"Then more of us shall come."

I pause in shock; their words send a bitter and unsettling chill up my spine. I swiftly realize I must do something before it's too late. These aliens will continue to take over—not just my hometown, possibly the whole world. *Who knows what could become of the world should there be more than just these few aliens?* I think. I start backing out of the room. Somehow, I've got to stop this madness and put these diabolical aliens' plan to an end.

Suddenly, the three aliens in dark suits become six, then twelve, and they reach for me as I run out into the basement warehouse. They grab hold of me; I can see them continuing to multiply. So many of these beings in dark suits now reach for me, but I fight them off. Tugging and pulling with all my strength, I wrestle free from their grasp, and I run out into the warehouse.

They are right behind me. I can see them multiplying, duplicating right before my eyes. There is no escape in sight. *What can I do against such astronomical odds?* I wonder.

As I run through the aisles of people lying on tables and bunched together in groups, with their cold, blank expressions, i feel both angry and afraid. They seem to stretch on forever. The fear reminds me I need to run. *I have to save everybody; I have to fight!* I say to myself.

In the dim light of the warehouse, I can see the men in suits everywhere, and they're closing in on me. I quickly duck to my knees and crawl beneath the tables full of people. I can feel my shins and knees begin to ache, but my adrenaline keeps me going. I must circle back and stop the machine. *That infernal thing must be what is keeping everyone unconscious. I have to shut it down and stop these creatures from taking over the world.*

I think I've lost them, I think.

From my vantage point, hidden underneath endless rows of tables, I can see shadows pass by. Hundreds of beings in dark suits run through the warehouse, desperately searching for me. With the looming presence of danger, quiet and alone, I can feel something in my chest, saying, *Get up. Move! Run, Evyn!*

My heart pounds with a sudden surge of energy. My hands and legs burn and sweat with newfound strength. My adrenaline kicks in again with a sudden burst of courage. As the last of the dark shadows fades out of sight in the warehouse, I quickly rise from my hiding spot. As fast as I can, I sneak back through the darkness of the vast room, heading straight for the machine.

I quietly approach the luminous room holding the alien machine. Following the cables and wires from the warehouse and from all the citizens of Newport, I realize that the tubes and pulsating wires connected to everyone converge here, in the machine. I take notice of the machine the aliens are working on. Three figures still reside within the room, tampering with the strange contraption as if it were the most important thing in the world. It is encased in shiny metal panels, curved and seamless. It has a lot of lights and electrical wires running everywhere. One large connecting wire seems to supply the machine with power.

I get the simplest idea and act on it without thinking. I make a break for the large socket in the wall. The aliens quickly rush to stop me. They cry out with the shrillest and most hypnotic voices.

"Stop!"

"What are you doing?"

"You must not stop the machine!"

I make it but a few steps inside the small room, but it's all I need to reach the alien machine. Two of the figures quickly swirl about and lunge at me. The alien beings grab hold of me, pulling with all their might to keep me from unplugging their precious machine, but it is too late. I have a firm grip on the large wire which is powering the machine.

I try with all my might to pull the plug from its socket, but it is locked tightly in place. I get my feet pressed firmly against the wall, with the aliens pulling on me, feebly attempting to stop what is about to happen. I grit my teeth and push with all my weight against the wall. My hands burn from the electrified heat coming from the wire. I clench my body through the pain and pull with one last surge of dying strength. As sparks fly, I can feel the plug coming free from the locked socket.

As if connected to the device's power, the aliens' mysterious source of energy, the alien beings lose all their strength. Their hold on me weakens, and they release me. I drop to the floor, my hands writhing in agony. The complex machine, with all sorts of lights, monitors, electrical tubes, and power cords extending into the large room full of unconscious people, winds down. The machine emits sparks and sputters fluid. The blinking lights and array of bright wires all go out. The once-shiny metal panels turn molten and pulsate with a dark, glowing light.

Two of the aliens in dark suits fall to the ground as they reach for me, leaving nothing but two piles of clothes on the ground. The last alien slumps away from the machine in a painful and contorted slouch. He looks up at me, now standing in front of him. In an almost-thankful and -relieved tone, the alien gives me one last farewell warning. "Thank you, Evyn Hunter. We were growing tired of this dimension's energy. We will meet again."

The alien disappears into his clothes; the dark suit and heavy overcoat fall into a pile on the floor. All of a sudden, a blue light glows from each mound of clothes. Small blue orbs of energy rise up out of the clothes. The swirling orbs are mesmerizing. They linger for just a moment, hovering right in front of me, lighting up my eyes in a brilliant blue spectrum of dazzling light. I feel stuck in some sort of a trance for a moment before the colorful orbs quickly vanish through the ceiling and off into the sky.

All the other men in dark suits, scattered throughout the mall and the city, start to disappear, leaving behind empty clothes, large hats, and black sunglasses. As Sam and Chloe drive through the city near the mall, they can't believe their eyes, as all the men they are trying so desperately to escape from begin to simply disappear.

I stand alone in the room, shocked and amazed at my first—and hopefully last—experience with actual aliens. I feel a soft vibration under my feet. The metal ceiling makes an unsettling, squeaking noise as the cement floors and brick walls rattle and vibrate. The large machine rumbles, violently shaking the room. I look around, scared, knowing this is definitely not a good sign.

The device lets off big, bright sparks and explodes from within. All of a sudden, the monitors and electric tubes burst into flames. The large alien machine begins to implode. Crumpling and twisting metal parts fold over themselves and bolts pop in a screaming show of sparks flying in all directions.

Over and over, the contraption turns and spins, and the room rumbles like an earthquake. The alien machine gets smaller and spins faster, hovering in the air as the rumbling vibrations get louder and stronger. I back out of the room as I throw my arms up to shield myself from the blinding flashes of blue and white light that shoot out in all directions. No larger than a baseball, the machine continues to shrink even smaller. A dazzling, swirling, blue-and-white orb spins faster and faster as it shrinks to the size of a marble.

Standing in the warehouse, still surrounded by the blinding light of this alien implosion, I get knocked off my feet as the ground beneath me vibrates powerfully. Then the machine lets out one last explosive bang, which echoes throughout the shopping mall. The device suddenly vanishes, and everything goes silent.

As I make my way out of the warehouse, I can see the people stirring and waking up. I want nothing more than to find my parents in the vast sea of people, but letting Chloe and Sam know that everything is okay is my first priority.

I head toward the large loading-bay doors. When I unlock one of them and swing the heavy door up on its rails, it slides open on the enormous tracks, letting in the cool breeze and the bright light of the setting sun. Then, as I open another of the massive loading-bay doors, letting in the bright, warm California sunshine, I look back to see all the people waking up and making their way toward the blinding light.

I hop down through the large garage doors, landing outside on the pavement of the mall parking lot. I make my way out of the parking lot, dialing Chloe's number on my cell phone. Sam and Chloe, who wait patiently nearby with their stolen getaway car, can see me walking up as Chloe reaches for her ringing cell phone. Chloe instantly runs full speed into me with a smile, throwing her arms around me and squeezing tightly. She is overjoyed to see that I am all right.

"Are you okay? What did you do?" Chloe blurts out, her watery eyes tearing up.

"It's a long story. I'm still trying to believe it myself," I vaguely reply.

"Hey, lovebirds, take a look!" Walking up nearby, Sam exclaims as he points to the shopping mall.

Chloe and I turn our heads to see hundreds upon hundreds of groggy and confused Newport residents making their way into the parking lot. Chloe, Sam, and I cheerfully smile with relief that this crazy ordeal is finally over.

CHAPTER 10

CONCLUSIONS

I wake up at home to an empty house. In a rush, I frantically search the house for my parents. After a moment of worry and shouting for my mom and dad, my dad calls out to me from the front entrance. It brings welcome relief, as I have not heard his voice in days.

"Evyn, we're home!"

In excitement, I run to the door to greet my parents with a big hug. They drop several bags of groceries and look at me curiously.

My dad continues. "Hey there, what's gotten into you? Strangest thing; all of a sudden, there was no food in the house."

I share a long-missed and normal hello with my father, who has no recollection of the "business trip" he was supposed to have been on for the last few days. Even my mom remembers he was on a trip, but she also can't remember anything about the last few days. When we're alone, all she quietly says to me is, "We need to talk after school, young man."

Outside, I notice that everything seems back to normal. The sun is shining, and the neighbors are out watering their flowers and mowing their lawns. People walk down the street with their kids and pets. People drive by with friendly waves, and walkers say hello as they pass by. I walk to Main Street, where businesses are open as usual. Everything is clean and normal, as if nothing unusual happened.

But the biggest relief waits just down the street, strolling slowly toward me. Chloe—with a great big smile on her face—sees me at the same time as I see her. We walk toward each other, and I can't help but crack a big smile as well.

"Everything seems to be back to normal around here."

"Yeah, no one remembers anything that happened."

"My parents don't know anything about the last few days."

"It's probably for the best."

"No one's going to know what you did for them—for the whole town."

"Well, I'm still not even 100 percent sure what I did." I pause for a moment and continue. "At least *you* know, and that's what's important." I smile, and Chloe throws her arms around me, quietly thanking me again for everything.

"Come on; let's get to school."

Everything at school also seems to have returned to normal. The long lines of yellow school buses line up outside the school. The crowds of students and teachers have returned, and they begin making their way inside.

Sir Arthur Wilfred High School is having track-and-field tryouts after school, and I decide to give it a shot. I line up alongside older boys, track stars, and supposedly much faster boys for the hundred-meter dash. They all snicker and chuckle.

"Hey, Ev, the girls' tryouts aren't until tomorrow!" The older bully who harassed me days ago pipes up, and everybody laughs at me, like usual.

I just crack a small, confident grin. I think back to all the running I have done over the last few days. I remember that spark of adrenaline I have become so accustomed to. The starting gun fires and I blast off. My adrenaline and confidence ignite, as they have so many times recently. Faster than I ever expected, my legs shoot out, one foot in front of the other, and I fly across the field, leaving everyone behind.

After a long day of school, I return home. The most daunting task now lies ahead of me—more challenging than anything else a young man should ever have to face, more complicated than dealing with high school bullies or taking on eighth grade, more difficult than trying to save my friends from a secret alien invasion, more terrifying than having to face off against an army of mysterious aliens in dark suits, and more confusing than rescuing an entire town from the clutches of ruthless mastermind aliens.

I must now attempt the most impossible thing I can possibly imagine: I have to try to explain everything that has happened … to my mom.

Evyn Hunter and the Secret Invasion

Be sure to watch for the next exciting adventures
featuring Evyn Hunter—coming soon!

Evyn Hunter versus the Zombie Curse

and

Evyn Hunter Visits the Other Realm